W9-BED-404

Dear Parents:

Congratulations! Your child is taking the first steps on an exciting journey. The destination? Independent reading!

STEP INTO READING® will help your child get there. The program offers five steps to reading success. Each step includes fun stories and colorful art or photographs. In addition to original fiction and books with favorite characters, there are Step into Reading Non-Fiction Readers, Phonics Readers and Boxed Sets, Sticker Readers, and Comic Readers—a complete literacy program with something to interest every child.

Learning to Read, Step by Step!

Ready to Read **Preschool–Kindergarten**
• big type and easy words • rhyme and rhythm • picture clues
For children who know the alphabet and are eager to begin reading.

Reading with Help **Preschool–Grade 1**
• basic vocabulary • short sentences • simple stories
For children who recognize familiar words and sound out new words with help.

Reading on Your Own **Grades 1–3**
• engaging characters • easy-to-follow plots • popular topics
For children who are ready to read on their own.

Reading Paragraphs **Grades 2–3**
• challenging vocabulary • short paragraphs • exciting stories
For newly independent readers who read simple sentences with confidence.

Ready for Chapters **Grades 2–4**
• chapters • longer paragraphs • full-color art
For children who want to take the plunge into chapter books but still like colorful pictures.

STEP INTO READING® is designed to give every child a successful reading experience. The grade levels are only guides; children will progress through the steps at their own speed, developing confidence in their reading.

Remember, a lifetime love of reading starts with a single step!

For Ashley Emma,
who makes the world
a better place
—C.B.C.

RHUS36575

 Published in the United States by Random House Children's Books, a division of Penguin Random House LLC, 1745 Broadway, New York, NY 10019, and in Canada by Penguin Random House Canada Limited, Toronto.

Visit us on the Web!
StepIntoReading.com
randomhousekids.com
dckids.kidswb.com

Educators and librarians, for a variety of teaching tools, visit us at RHTeachersLibrarians.com

ISBN 978-0-399-55344-8 (trade)
ISBN 978-0-399-55345-5 (lib. bdg.)
ISBN 978-0-399-55346-2 (ebook)

Printed in the United States of America
10 9 8 7 6 5 4 3 2 1

STEP INTO READING®

SUPERGIRL TAKES OFF!

by Courtney Carbone

illustrated by Erik Doescher

Random House New York

Meet Supergirl!
Her real name
is Kara Zor-El.
She is a super hero!

Supergirl grew up
on a planet far,
far from Earth.

But her planet
was not stable.
It was about to explode!

Supergirl's family wanted to keep her safe.

They sent her
to live on Earth
with her cousin,
Superman!

Superman was happy
to see Supergirl.
He showed her
around Metropolis,
the city he called home.

As she got older,
Supergirl's powers
began to grow.
She had super-strength,

super-speed,

and X-ray vision!

Supergirl's heat vision
can melt anything.

Her super-breath can blow the villains away!

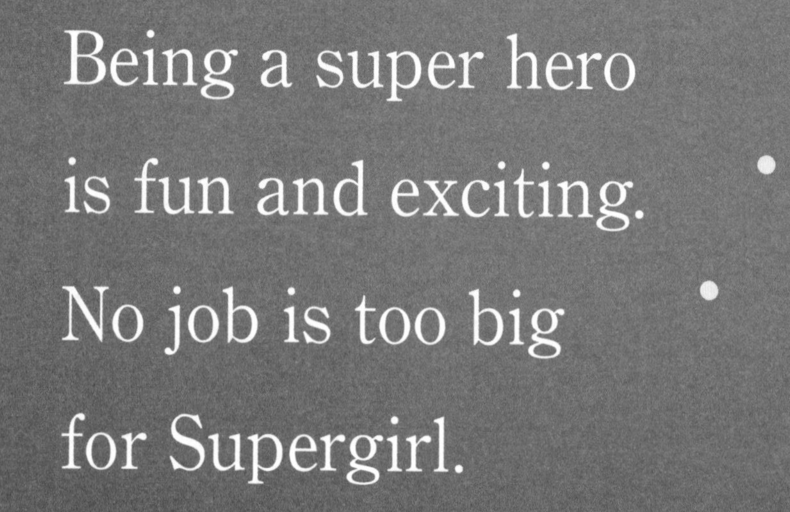

Being a super hero
is fun and exciting.
No job is too big
for Supergirl.

Her Super-Cat,
Streaky,
has powers, too!

Supergirl joins
the Super Friends
to stop villains
like Poison Ivy.

Supergirl has to be
on the lookout
for danger.

Bad guys are always threatening Earth.

Fighting crime is
a full-time job!
Supergirl is up
for the challenge.

Supergirl takes off.

She will save the day!